First published in
North America by Annick Press 2003
Text © 2002 Meg Clibbon
Illustrations © 2002 Lucy Clibbon
Originally published by Zero to Ten Limited
(a member of the Evans Publishing Group)
© 2002 Zero to Ten Limited

Cataloging in Publication
Clibbon, Meg
Imagine you're a mermaid! / text by Meg Clibbon ; illustrations by Lucy Clibbon.
-- North American ed.
(Imagine this! series)
ISBN 1-55037-791-4 (bound).--ISBN 1-55037-790-6 (pbk.)
1. Mermaids--Juvenile literature. I. Clibbon, Lucy II. Title.
III. Series: Clibbon, Meg. Imagine this! series.
GR910.C55 2003   j398'.45   C2002-905207-6

Distributed in Canada and the U.S.A. by Firefly Books Ltd.
www.annickpress.com
Printed in China

Imagine you're a
Mermaid!

Mer Meg
(also know as
Meg Clibbon)
Although Mer Meg is
not a mermaid, she is a
sea friend. Sea friends
know all about where mermaids
live and play and they try to help them if they
can. Mer Meg loves beachcombing and
pebble-hunting with her family and other
sea friends.

Lorelei Lucy
(also know as
Lucy Clibbon)
lives in a magical
land far, far away.
It is surrounded by soft
sandy beaches, clear blue waters, and
exotic sea creatures. She has had some
wonderful adventures with a real mermaid
family who have inspired her
paintings for this book.

With special love and thanks to:
two beautiful mermaids, Ella and Rosa

What is a mermaid?

A mermaid is
a legendary creature
who has the body of
a woman and
the tail of a fish.

What do mermaids look like?

Mermaids are very beautiful, but it is hard work being beautiful and they spend a lot of time looking after their appearance.

They sleep with sea cucumbers on their eyelids.

They polish their scales with silver seaweed.

They clean their teeth with powdered coral and pearl.

They brush their hair with sweet-smelling oils to remove salt water.

Mermaids do not lead very useful lives.
They are mainly decorative.

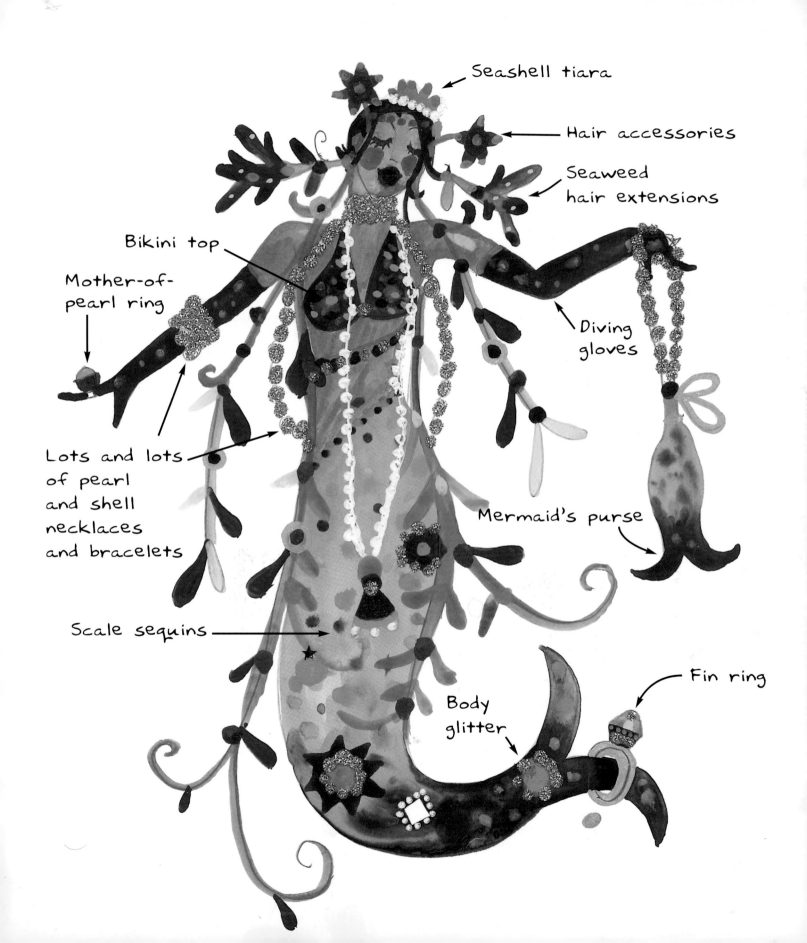

Seashell tiara

Hair accessories

Seaweed hair extensions

Bikini top

Mother-of-pearl ring

Diving gloves

Lots and lots of pearl and shell necklaces and bracelets

Mermaid's purse

Scale sequins

Fin ring

Body glitter

Life under the sea

Mer-babies come ready-made in beautiful eggs
made of mother-of-pearl. They live inside their eggs until
they grow too big and then they use them
to keep all their special things in.

Mer-babies
are looked after
by sea horses, who are
the nursemaids
of the sea.

Mermaids love their babies very much,
but they do not make very good mothers because they spend
too much time combing their seaweed green hair
and playing with pirates to trick them out of their treasure.

Mermen are fierce and strong and they
spend a lot of their time sharpening their tridents
and chasing away pirates.
Neptune is the king of the sea. He lives in his palace
deep in the deepest ocean.
Every morning he rides his chariot across the waves
to work, and every evening he rides it back home again.

What do mermaids do?

Mermaids love causing mischief and playing tricks.
They play with their catfish and take their dogfish for walks –
perhaps this is better than being useful!

Mermaids love to have parties.
They send out invitations by mer-mail
and go shopping in the mer-market
for delicious things to eat.

Mer-party menu

Crispy seaweed
Sponge cake, Mer-ingues
Coral cordial

Then the mermaids spend ages
decorating the rocks and seabed
(and, of course, they spend yet
more time making themselves
look beautiful).

Why don't you plan a mermaid party?

Where do mermaids live?

You are not very likely
to see mermaids because they
only live in sparkling bright water,
and wherever human beings live
the water is spoiled.
Mermaids live in coral castles with
turrets of pearl. Their gardens are full of
sea anemones and swaying seaweed.
They keep brittle starfish and
sea urchins as pets, and
all around the rocks swim
rainbow-colored fish.

Merry Mermaid Day

*O*nce a year, Neptune summons all the mermaids and mermen to a special party.

1. *The Sole Sisters win the singing competition.*
2. *Mermaids, mermen, and mer-babies love to swim around the mer-pole.*
3. *Mer-babies love the egg-and-spoon races.*

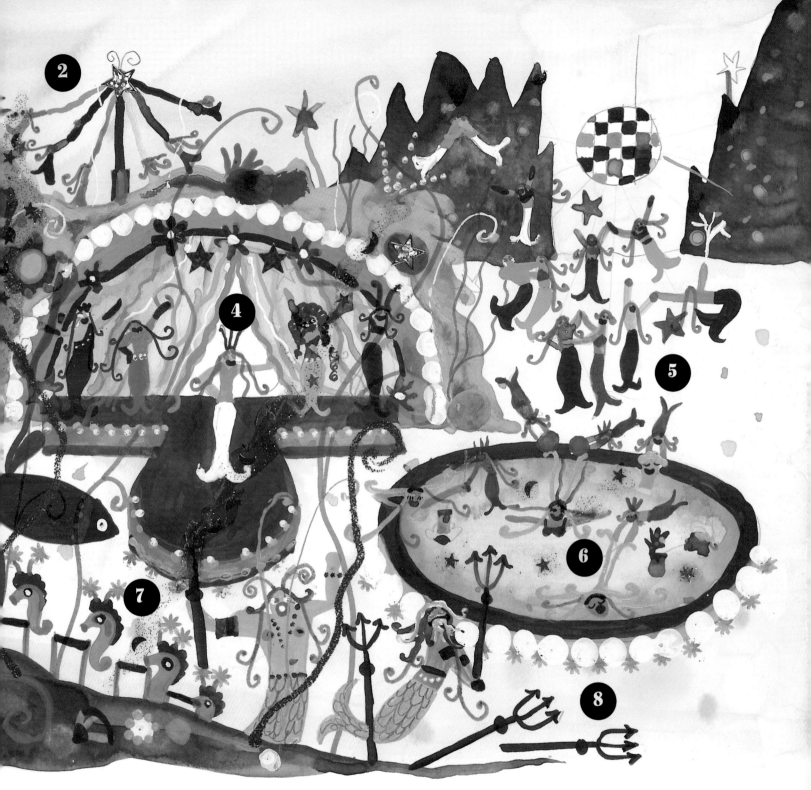

4. *All the mermaids enjoy the Miss Atlantis Beauty Pageant.*

5. *Everyone likes to get down to Fat Buoy Swim.*

6. *Mermaids get their hair styled and nails polished in the pampering pool.*

7. *Sea horse hurdles are great fun.*

8. *Tossing the trident is a popular competition.*

Sea scenes

Mermaids live in a beautiful sea world.
Underwater the sea is aquamarine, but when the sun
shines through, it changes to turquoise
with deep green shadows.

*Near coral reefs, the sea is multicolored
like the fish swimming about.*

When it is cold, the mermaids like to catch a lift from whales and dolphins traveling north. They sit on great crystal icebergs wearing jackets knitted out of polar bear wool and watch the northern lights.

On clear nights, the sea is black with silver ripples. The mermaids float on their backs and look at the stars.

Perhaps you can paint your own picture of a sea world?

Mermaid communication

Mermaids used to communicate by
singing or by sea-snail mail. But now they are really
into modern communication. They used to surf
the sea, now they surf the Net.

Shell phone

Sea D
drive

You can listen to a shell phone too –
find a large shell and hold it to your ear.
You will hear the sea and perhaps,
far away, a mermaid singing.

Writing to a mermaid

Seashell Cottage
24 Shingle Lane
Rockminster

Dear Mermaid,

Every morning I take my dog Ben for a walk on the beach. He always goes mad but yesterday he just stopped all of a sudden. Then I knew why, because I heard this noise. It was a nice noise, but sad. Suddenly I saw you. You were sitting on a rock with your tail in the sea, singing. Why were you there? Why were you sad?

I don't see how you can be, because you are so pretty and the sea is so beautiful. Please will you write to me. I will leave this letter in a shell on your rock.

Love from
William Budd

Why don't you write back to William
or contact the mermaid yourself on

MerMeg-Underwater @ madasafish.com

Decorations and accessories

Mermaids love decoration.
They weave pearls and precious stones into their hair.
(All mermaids have seaweed green hair,
but of course many of them dye it!)
They make necklaces and bangles threaded
with different kinds of shells.
They sew shawls and scarves made out of
the finest ribbon seaweed, which
they drape around themselves.
Their fish tails are studded with gold and jewelry
stolen from pirate treasure.
They sit on rocks and gaze at their own reflection in
looking glasses made from starlight and seafoam.

Seaweed shampoo

Mother-of-pearl ring

Scale polish

Makeup

Lots of different mirrors

Shell outfit

Hair accessories

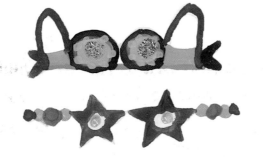

Bikini tops

Brushes

Scale glitter and sequins

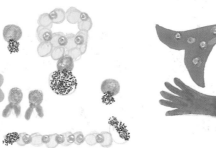

Jewelry

Mermaid gloves

Mysteries of the sea

Long ago, when sailors went to sea in sailing ships,
the world was full of mysterious places that had never been
discovered. Sailors spent many months away from home,
eating ship's biscuits and drinking grog. This affected their eyesight.
When they caught glimpses of unusual sea creatures,
they thought they were seeing mermaids and sea monsters
– but they were probably seals and manatees.

The Moha-moha

lives off the coast of New Zealand. It has a huge
shell and snapping jaws. It sounds bad.

Sea Serpents

are said to appear out of the deepest water
and twist and twine themselves around
small boats. They sound very bad.

The Kraken

is thought to be an enormous squid with giant tentacles,
and is as big as a small island. It sounds frightful. Help!

**Could these stories be true?
The mermaids know, but they won't tell.**

Famous mermaids

There are many stories of mermaids who sit on
rocks singing beautiful songs.
Sailors hearing this enchanted music forgot
what they were supposed to be doing.
They would crash into the rocks and then
their ships would float down to the bottom of
the sea, where they would belong to the mermaids
for the rest of time.

The Little Mermaid

by Hans Christian Andersen is one of the saddest fairy tales.
In it, the Little Mermaid (who is very beautiful)
falls in love with a human prince whom she rescues from a shipwreck.

She goes to visit the Sea Witch, and in exchange for her lovely voice
she is given a potion that will change her tail into human legs
so she can live on land with the prince. But without
her voice, she cannot tell him that she was the one who rescued him
and how much she loves him … so he marries someone else.

Drinking strange potions from Sea Witches (or anyone else)
is always a bad idea. Most mermaids don't! They live happy lives
swimming and singing … and working hard at being beautiful!

Things to do

Pebble collection

Collect shells and pebbles from the beach.
Place them in a large glass jar
and fill with fresh water. This looks lovely
on a sunny window ledge.

Shell decorations

Use little shells to decorate
small boxes, picture frames, or mirrors.
First, cover your box or frame
with plaster, then press the shells
carefully into it while it is still damp.
When the plaster is dry,
you can varnish or paint the shells.

Dress up as a mermaid

Weave beads and shells and ribbons
into your hair. Dress up in sea-colored
clothes and pretend that your legs
are a tail by putting
body glitter on.

Coral cordial

You will need:
orange juice
pink food coloring
marshmallows

Directions

1. Fill a jug almost full with orange juice.
2. Add one small drop of color and stir well.
3. Float chopped marshmallows on top.

Mer-ingues

For two portions you will need:
4 store-bought meringues
whipped cream
1 drop of blue and
1 drop of green food coloring
1 star fruit or crystallized angelica

Directions

1. Break the meringues into bits.
2. Swirl the food coloring gently into
the cream and add to the meringues.
3. Spoon into pretty dishes and
decorate with pieces
of star fruit or angelica.